Beak & Ally
Unlikely Friends

Norm Feuti

HARPER alley

An Imprint of HarperCollins Publishers

To all my friends, likely or otherwise.

6

8

10

11

14

15

I used to live next to a bird with no sense of humor.

What do you get when you cross an elephant with a centipede?

I told him jokes all the time, but he never laughed.

A monster! Ha ha ha!

I didn't give up, though. I kept trying, day after day.

Until he moved away suddenly.

21

25

26

27

Three

What the...

47

That bird is
a Long-Billed
Party Pooper.
They don't
build their
own nests.

They wait for a smaller bird
to finish building one...

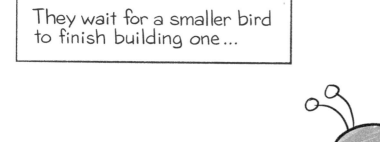

... then kick them out.

Leaving that bird's nest-warming party officially pooped.

HarperAlley is an imprint of HarperCollins Publishers.

Beak & Ally #1: Unlikely Friends
Copyright © 2021 by Norm Feuti
All rights reserved. Manufactured in Canada.
No part of this book may be used or reproduced in any manner whatsoever without
written permission except in the case of brief quotations embodied in critical
articles and reviews. For information address HarperCollins Children's Books, a
division of HarperCollins Publishers, 195 Broadway, New York, NY 10007.
www.harperalley.com

Library of Congress Control Number: 2020937706
ISBN 978-0-06-302157-0 (hardcover) — ISBN 978-0-06-302158-7 (pbk.)

Typography by Norm Feuti
22 23 24 25 26   TC   10 9 8 7 6 5 4

First Edition